Rubens

Rembrandt

GREAT ARTISTS

by DOROTHY AITCHISON
with illustrations by MARTIN AITCHISON

Vermeer

Publishers:
Ladybird Books Ltd . Loughborough

Printed in England

Rubens (1577-1640)

Peter Paul Rubens, was born in 1577. His family came from Antwerp, which is in that part of the Low Countries which we now call Belgium.

In those days, Holland and Belgium were a collection of separate provinces under Spanish rule, and the people were beginning to rebel against their oppressors. Rubens' father had to escape to Germany from the Spaniards, and it was there, in a little town called Siegen, that Rubens was born. Until he was nine he lived in Cologne with his parents and his brother Philip. In 1587 his father died and his mother took the young brothers back to Antwerp.

Rubens went to school in Antwerp and learned Latin and Greek. His mother wanted him to be a courtier, and when he was thirteen she sent him to be a page in the court of an elderly princess, Marguerite de Ligne. This was not a very interesting life for a young boy who was already beginning to show signs of a talent for drawing.

Rubens asked his mother to take him away from court, and in 1591 he was sent to study with a landscape painter named Tobias Verhaecht. After six months he went to work with another artist, Adam Van Noort, and Rubens spent four years in this artist's rather rough and lively studio. His third teacher was a much-travelled and clever man named Otto Van Veen, and Rubens worked in his studio until 1600.

Peter Paul Rubens finds life as a page boy very boring.

7214 0254 2

Rubens was a handsome young man, tall and fair-haired. He knew Latin and Greek, and learned to speak French, Italian and Spanish as well as his own language, which was Flemish.

In 1600, when he was twenty-three, Rubens set out for Italy, where most of the great painters had lived. In Venice he met the Duke of Mantua and became his court painter. They travelled together to Florence, where Rubens was able to study the work of great Renaissance artists such as Michelangelo, Leonardo da Vinci and Raphael.

In Florence, Rubens made a copy of Leonardo da Vinci's famous cartoon, or drawing, "*The Battle of Anghiari*". The cartoon was later lost, and Rubens' drawing is the only record we have of that great work. He also made copies of several paintings by Raphael, who had died nearly a hundred years earlier.

Rubens then went to Spain for the Duke of Mantua, taking presents to the King. He took pictures and other gifts which included a coach and six bay horses. He had "twenty days of tiresome travel with daily rain and violent winds." Some of the paintings were damaged by the weather.

Rubens stayed with the Duke of Mantua for eight years. He became a very great painter and familiar with court life. In 1608 his mother became ill, and he hurried home, but he was unable to reach Antwerp before she died.

Rain and wind spoil some of the pictures being taken by Rubens to the King of Spain.

After his mother's death, Rubens did not go back to Italy but stayed in Antwerp. The city had suffered greatly in the wars between Spain and the Netherlands, and the Dutch had closed the River Scheldt. This meant that there was little trade and few people in the city. There was even grass growing in the streets.

The rulers, or Stadholders, were a Spanish princess, Isabella, and her husband, Albert. They welcomed Rubens, and offered him the position of court painter with a salary of five hundred florins. Rubens accepted on condition that he was allowed to live in Antwerp and not at the court in Brussels.

In 1609, Rubens married Isabella Brandt, an intelligent girl of good family; she was eighteen years of age and made Rubens very happy. He often painted her, and in one picture they are seen together, beautifully dressed and against the honeysuckle which bloomed in their garden.

Rubens bought a fine house in Antwerp, and enlarged it. He made an Italian garden, with low hedges and trees in pots. He also built a large studio and a triumphal arch. There was also a gallery in the shape of a semi-circle, where his collection of statues was displayed.

Rubens was a great success in Antwerp, and many people came to his studio. He worked very hard all day, and often when he was tired he mounted his horse and enjoyed a ride along the banks of the River Scheldt.

Rubens paints Isabella and himself in the honeysuckle bower in their garden.

Rubens was by now so famous that many young artists wanted to work with him, and in 1611 he had to refuse a hundred would-be pupils.

Rubens' name is on so many pictures that he could not possibly have painted them all by himself. The only works which we can be sure are entirely his, are the small oil sketches he made for his very large paintings. His method was to make a sketch and then allow his pupils to draw out the large picture and work on it. Rubens then added the finishing touches and signed the picture.

Rubens trained his pupils to paint all the birds, animals, fishes and flowers in his paintings, and also the forests, landscapes and streams. One of the pupils was Anthony Van Dyck, who later became a famous artist in England.

Rubens is described as painting, receiving visitors, being read to, and dictating a letter all at the same time. No wonder he once said, "I am the busiest and most harassed man on earth."

Rubens' fame was spread by engravings and woodcuts of his pictures. This made his work known to people who could not see the actual original paintings. However, he had trouble with his engraver, who insisted that the prints were popular because of his own fine engraving and not because they were Rubens' paintings.

Rubens was a fine administrator, and his picture factory provided work for artists who might not have succeeded on their own.

Rubens looks at some work by Anthony Van Dyck, whom he regarded as the most talented of the artists he employed in his picture factory.

At that time, France, Spain, England and the Low Countries were all seeking power, yet each wished to avoid war. Because of this situation, Rubens had the opportunity to become a diplomat as well as a painter. He was trusted and everybody liked him, so he was able to travel, outwardly as an artist but really as a representative of the rulers of his country.

Rubens went several times to Paris, to decorate the Luxembourg Palace with scenes from the life of the Queen Mother. There he met French politicians as well as the English Duke of Buckingham.

In 1622 the Stadholder, Albert, died, and Isabella relied more and more on Rubens, making him a Noble and a Gentleman of the Royal Household.

Rubens was sent to Spain on a diplomatic mission, and even then managed to continue his painting. He met the great Spanish artist, Velazquez, and made a journey with him to the mountains outside Madrid. He also painted portraits of the Spanish royal family.

In 1626 Rubens' wife, Isabella Brandt, died of the plague. Rubens tried to forget his sorrow by concentrating on his political work, but he was often weary of the treachery of the courtiers and sad that he had to spend so much time away from his young sons, Albert and Nicholas, a picture of whom can be seen in the National Gallery in London.

 Rubens and Velazquez in the mountains near Madrid.

It is interesting to know that Rubens visited England. He was sent by the Spanish king, who still ruled over the Low Countries, to arrange for an exchange of ambassadors. Rubens was in England for nearly a year. He did not look forward to his visit because he thought the English were people who were always changing their minds. In time, however, he came to admire them, and King Charles I liked Rubens. He visited Cambridge University, and received a degree of Master of Arts. He was also knighted by Charles I, who tried to persuade him to work permanently at the English court.

Rubens painted a picture of St. George and the Dragon, which he presented to the King. St. George has the face of Charles I, and the princess, for whom St. George slayed the dragon, has the features of his wife, Henrietta Maria. In the background of the picture is a view of the Thames Valley.

When he returned from England, Rubens painted nine large pictures for the ceiling of the Palace of Whitehall. The pictures told the story of the life of James I. The panels did not fit properly, as Rubens had not calculated the measurements correctly in English feet. King Charles was very pleased with the ceiling, although he took a long time to pay for it. He ordered that no entertainments should take place in the Banqueting Hall for three years, in case the smoke from the candles should damage the paintings.

King Charles I knights Rubens.

By now Rubens was very tired of his diplomatic missions, and he begged the Infanta Isabella to let him stay in Antwerp and remain there in her employment.

Rubens decided to marry again, and for a wife he chose a sixteen year old girl, Hélène Fourment, who was the eleventh child of an Antwerp silk merchant. Because he was bored with court life, he deliberately chose a simple girl who, he said, "would not blush to see me take my brushes in my hand."

The Infanta Isabella died, and a brother of the Spanish king was chosen to rule the Netherlands. His entry into the city of Antwerp was made an occasion for public celebrations. Rubens was in charge of the decorations, and designed triumphal arches and ceremonial chariots. Decorated floats lined the route as Ferdinand approached the city by river. Musicians played and the people danced in the streets. Guns were fired and there was a firework display from the cathedral tower. Rubens was not present at the festivities. He was so exhausted by all the work he had done that he was ill in bed when the new ruler arrived.

Fireworks and processions celebrate the arrival of the Spanish ruler.

Rubens was no longer a courtier, but he was still a very busy painter, and he painted many more pictures for the King of Spain. However, he became weary of city life, and decided to live with his family in the Castle of Steen. This large mansion still stands in the country north of Antwerp. Rubens was Lord of the Manor, and bought forests and land around the house.

We can see in Rubens' paintings how these looked in his time. The castle had a drawbridge and a moat, a lake and farm-buildings. In his pictures however, Rubens surrounds it with valleys and distant hills although the countryside is really very flat. He always loved the past, and one picture of the house shows knights jousting in front of the drawbridge.

Rubens was court painter to Ferdinand, but worked and lived quietly in the country with his wife Hélène and their four little children. Rubens had suffered for some years from attacks of gout, and his hands became more and more crippled by the disease. He died in 1640, and his last child, a daughter, was born after his death.

Rubens' work is famous for its rich colour and its magnificent drawing. His lively character made his paint flow freely, and his portraits sparkle with life. He is celebrated today as one of the really great artists of all time.

Rubens and his wife ride round their estate.

Rembrandt (1606-1669)

Rembrandt van Rijn was born at Leyden in Holland in 1606. In England at that time, Queen Elizabeth I had just died and Shakespeare was writing his plays. Holland had been fighting for her freedom from Spanish rule and was approaching a time of peace and great prosperity.

Rembrandt was the son of a miller, and his mother was a baker's daughter. He was the sixth of a family of seven children.

Leyden was, and still is, a famous old University city on the banks of the River Rhine, and from his window Rembrandt could see two windmills which belonged to his family. Beyond them was the busy river with its barges and sailing ships.

We do not know much about Rembrandt's childhood, but we know that he entered the Grammar School at Leyden when he was seven, and that when he was fourteen he entered the University. This was quite usual in those days. However, Rembrandt soon found that he was not suited to a life of learning, and asked his parents to allow him to become a painter.

Rembrandt's parents apprenticed him to an artist in Leyden, named Jacob van Swanenburgh, and the young man worked in his studio for three years. He learned to draw and paint in Leyden, but it was not until he went to Amsterdam in 1624 that Rembrandt met much-travelled and skilful painters. It was in Amsterdam that Rembrandt began his real career as an artist.

Young Rembrandt plays by the Rhine at Leyden, within view of the family windmills.

Most artists of Rembrandt's time used to go to Italy to study and to see the works of the great masters. Rembrandt never went there, but he learned a great deal about Italian painting from Pieter Lastman, his new teacher in Amsterdam.

He became interested in painting biblical scenes, especially from the Old Testament, and in using the very strong lights and shadows which make Rembrandt's work so easy to recognise. He used to draw and paint the people of Amsterdam, and some of the characters in his biblical pictures are shown wearing the clothes of Dutch people of Rembrandt's day.

Amsterdam was becoming a great city, and was replacing Antwerp as the chief port of northern Europe. After working with Lastman, Rembrandt went back to Leyden for a short while but soon returned to Amsterdam, never to leave the city again.

In 1631, when Rembrandt was twenty-five, he painted a picture which made him famous. It is called "*The Anatomy Lesson*," and shows a group of Dutch doctors seated round the body of a dead man, with their professor, Dr. Tulp, showing them the muscles of the arm. This was quite a new way of painting a portrait group. Previously, the doctors would probably have been depicted standing stiffly in a row. People became interested in this new artist, and went to Rembrandt to have their portraits painted.

Rembrandt arrives to make sketches for his painting, "The Anatomy Lesson."

Rembrandt preferred to paint portraits of his friends, the doctors, lawyers and learned Jews who lived in Amsterdam, but about this time he began to paint pictures of rich and important people.

Rembrandt was not a handsome young man; we know what he looked like from the many self-portraits which he painted during his life. He had a large nose, thick lips and untidy hair, and it was said that he used to wipe his oil-paint brushes on his clothes. He was, however, rather extravagant and liked dressing-up in fine costumes. He was very interested in old-fashioned clothes, which he collected and hung in his studio.

When Rembrandt settled in Amsterdam, he lived in the house of an art-dealer named Ullenborsch. This man kept a school where young people learned to paint by copying pictures. Here Rembrandt met Saskia Ullenborsch, the dealer's cousin. Saskia was an orphan who came from an important and distinguished family, and her father had left her a considerable fortune.

Saskia and Rembrandt were married in 1634, and were very happy. Rembrandt painted a picture of Saskia dressed in beautiful Eastern robes and with flowers in her hair. He also painted a picture of himself, laughing and drinking, with Saskia on his knee.

He was now a fashionable painter who could charge large sums of money for his work. All he and Saskia needed was a fine house to live in.

Painting a picture of himself and Saskia, Rembrandt absentmindedly wipes his brush on his clothes.

The house that Rembrandt bought in Amsterdam may still be seen, although it has been altered a great deal. It is near the River Amstel, and when Rembrandt and Saskia went there it was almost new.

Rembrandt was a great collector, and at auction sales bought many beautiful things which could later be painted into his pictures. As well as costumes, he bought armour, knives and sabres, musical instruments, and pictures and engravings by other artists.

Rembrandt's possessions were very important to him; there is a story about him wanting to make a record of his pet monkey which had died. As he had no other canvas prepared he insisted on painting it into the picture of a rich couple who were sitting for their portraits at the time. Naturally enough the couple did not want a monkey, dead or alive, in their picture, and indignantly left the studio. Rembrandt kept the picture and used it as a partition in his workroom.

Rembrandt's house was very expensive, and he could not afford to pay for it completely. Although he was paid large sums of money for his pictures, and Saskia brought him a handsome dowry, he was troubled by a shortage of money for the rest of his life.

A wealthy couple refuse to let Rembrandt paint a picture of his pet monkey into their portrait.

Troubles soon began to crowd in upon Rembrandt. His mother died, and of four children born to him, only one lived for more than a few months. Very many children died in infancy in those days.

After his son, Titus, was born, Saskia became ill, and she died in 1642. She left half her money to Rembrandt and half to her son. Her will stated that should Rembrandt marry again, his share of the money must go back to her family.

In spite of his sorrow, Rembrandt painted his most famous work during the year of Saskia's death. This is called "*The Night Watch*," and half a million people go every year to see it in the Rijksmuseum in Amsterdam. This picture is of a company of militia in Amsterdam, a company which had gradually lost its military character and become almost a social club. As with "*The Anatomy Lesson*," Rembrandt did not paint a formal portrait group, but even included children and dogs in his picture. Each person posed separately and paid towards the cost in proportion to the prominence given to his portrait in the painting.

Because of the strong lights and shadows, and because the picture has darkened with age, it is called "*The Night Watch*," but it is really a day-time scene. Its real name is "*Parade of the Civic Guard under Captain Frans Banning-Cocq.*"

An officer poses for his portrait in Rembrandt's great masterpiece – "The Night Watch."

As well as being celebrated as a painter in oils, Rembrandt was perhaps the greatest etcher of all time.

Etching, like engraving, is done on copper plates, and a number of prints can then be made from the plate. An engraver has to use a strong, steel tool which cuts the lines out of the copper, rather like lino-cutting. Etching is much quicker. First the plate is given a thin coat of wax, or varnish. Using a needle point, the artist then draws lightly, scratching only through the wax. The whole plate is then put into an acid bath. The acid can eat into the copper only where the wax has been scratched, so it eats, or "etches" the drawing into the copper plate. Etchings and engravings are both printed in the same way. Ink is dabbed all over the plate, which is then wiped, leaving ink only in the etched lines. This is then squeezed onto paper in a press. Rembrandt did many portraits, landscapes and biblical scenes in this medium. He never told people exactly how he made his etchings and many of his secrets died with him.

Rembrandt now developed a new interest in landscapes, and often walked miles along the River Amstel making drawings. He was never interested in new buildings. Ignoring the new Town Hall in Amsterdam, he drew the old one being demolished. He drew old mills and ruined churches, using pen and ink, and peopled his sketches with fishermen, boatmen and farm-workers, showing us the daily life of his time.

Rembrandt sketching the old Town Hall during demolition.

After Saskia's death, Rembrandt was unable to marry again because he would have lost the money that Saskia left him in her will. His companion in later life was Hendrikje Stoffels. She was the daughter of a sergeant, and not from such a wealthy and respected family as Saskia's. Hendrikje was Rembrandt's housekeeper, and nurse to his son Titus. She posed as a model for Rembrandt in several of his drawings and paintings.

Rembrandt was still extravagant and continued to enlarge his collection. He had never finished paying for his house, and by 1656 he was in very serious financial difficulties. His troubles were not settled for four years, and in the end all his treasures had to be sold.

A list was made of his possessions, which included hundreds of paintings and drawings as well as many statues. There were also helmets, cuirasses, crossbows, arrows and shields, as well as seven stringed musical instruments and thirteen bamboo wind instruments. Poor Rembrandt had to part with all of these, and with his lion skins, stags' horns and "forty-seven Sea Creatures." There was even a Bird of Paradise.

In 1660, Rembrandt had to leave the house to which he had brought Saskia as a bride, and he moved to a humbler dwelling on the other side of the city.

Rembrandt's collection is taken away for sale.

The Guild of St. Luke, which controlled the financial affairs of its members, no longer allowed him to sell his pictures, but Titus and Hendrikje acted as his agents and paid him for his work.

Rembrandt gave up painting large pictures and landscapes, but continued to paint portraits and to take pupils. People no longer admired his work, and somebody once complained that "the paint was so thick that if you laid the picture on the floor you could pick it up by the nose." We can see from his self-portraits that by the time he was sixty, Rembrandt had become an old man with silvery hair, wrinkled forehead and neglected clothes.

Most painters of Rembrandt's day worked at Court, painting fashionable pictures, but it was said of him that "when he was working he would not have granted audience to the first monarch of the world."

He had a most wonderful gift for revealing character, and his treatment of chiaroscuro, or light and shade, has never been equalled.

Rembrandt died in 1669, saddened by the death the year before, of his son Titus, who was only twenty-seven. At the time, his death was hardly noticed in Amsterdam, but he is recognised today as the greatest of all Dutch painters.

Old Rembrandt and Hendrikje Stoffels walk by the frozen river.

Vermeer (1632-1675)

Rubens and Rembrandt were the greatest of the Flemish and Dutch artists, but there were many others who are important in the history of art. Pieter Breughel (1525-1569) is known for his scenes of peasant life, and Sir Anthony Van Dyck (1599-1641), a pupil of Rubens, became famous as a portrait painter in England. Franz Hals (1580-1666) was another portrait painter, and is celebrated for his "*Laughing Cavalier*." This is to mention only three. In the seventeenth century, the great age of Dutch painting, one of the finest painters was Jan Vermeer of Delft.

Vermeer was born in 1632, the year that Rembrandt painted his "*Anatomy Lesson*," and Rubens had just returned from England. Very little is known about Vermeer's life. There are only a few records concerning him, and he left no diary or letters. He did not even paint any self-portraits so we cannot be sure what he looked like. In his picture "*A Painter in His Studio*," the artist is almost certainly Vermeer, but only his back view is showing. In another of his paintings there is a musician whom some experts think might be a self-portrait of Vermeer.

Vermeer's father, Reynier, was a silk-weaver and made tapestries for curtains and upholstery. He also kept a tavern, the "Mechelen," and ran an art dealer's business as well. With this variety of professions, we may assume that Reynier was able to bring up his son in reasonable security, and that from an early age the boy was probably in contact with the world of art.

The young Vermeer in his father's weaving and picture-dealing establishment.

Of Vermeer's schooldays we know nothing. His father, who probably designed his own tapestries, could no doubt have helped him in his early training as an artist. When Vermeer was twenty-one he became a Master, which means that he had served a six-year apprenticeship, but we do not know in whose studio he worked. One artist whose name has been suggested as Vermeer's teacher is Carel Fabritius, a pupil of Rembrandt, because when Fabritius was killed in the explosion of the powder magazine in Delft in 1654, it was said that ". . . the art of Fabritius would live on in Vermeer." Vermeer was then only a young man and unknown as an artist, so it sounds as if he was Fabritius' most promising pupil.

When Vermeer was twenty-three, he married Catharina Bolnes. They lived in his father's house, with its weaving workshop above the tavern, and where too, the art-dealing business was conducted.

Two years later, Vermeer's father died and the tavern and art-dealer's business became his own, so that at the age of twenty-three he was in an enviable position for any artist. The income from his two businesses could support his family and widowed mother, and leave him free to paint just as he wished.

All Vermeer's pictures are serene and dignified. This, and the very fact that there are no records of his life, suggest that although one of the greatest of artists, Jan Vermeer was not a remarkable personality. With Catharina and their eight children, he probably lived the happily domesticated life of any respected citizen of Delft.

Vermeer with his family.

Delft, like Leyden and Amsterdam, is an old city of canals and tree-lined streets. It has always been famous for its china, which is hand-painted with blue and white designs which early travellers brought back from the Far East.

From two paintings by Vermeer we can see very clearly what Delft was like three hundred years ago. One, the famous "*View of Delft*," shows the town across a canal, with its gatehouse, carillon tower, convents, and barges tied up against the quay. It is bathed in the pearly light which is typical of Holland, and is one of the most famous pictures of a town ever painted. Equally well-known is "*A Street in Delft*," which Vermeer painted from the window of his house. Here we see an old brick building across a cobbled street, and through whitewashed doorways women can be seen going about their work. The tiled pavements, leaded windows with painted shutters, and mellow brickwork are lovingly depicted. These are Vermeer's only outdoor paintings.

Delft was not a centre of artistic activity until, in Vermeer's time, several well-known artists settled there. Carel Fabritius, Paulus Potter, Peter de Hooch and Jan Steen amongst them. Like all other artists, Vermeer had joined the Guild of St. Luke, and the fact that he was twice made president shows that he was held in high esteem. However, this would most likely have been due to his reputation as an art-dealer and expert, since as an artist he was hardly known.

From his window, Vermeer paints the famous 'Street in Delft.'

Unlike the Italians, who painted religious pictures on the walls of their churches, Dutch and Flemish artists preferred to paint scenes from everyday life, or "*genre*" pictures, and portraits. Vermeer was no exception, and nearly all his paintings are "*genre*" pictures.

He was fond of painting his sitters with their musical instruments. There are two pictures of women playing the lute, and another shows a young lady with a guitar. Two famous pictures in the National Gallery in London show women at their virginals, a kind of spinet.* He shows us an astronomer with his globes and a geographer with his maps, but mostly we are given enchanting glimpses of Dutch housewives at their daily tasks. They make lace, write letters, try on pearls or work in their kitchens.

All these paintings are thought to have been painted in Vermeer's studio. The light comes from a high leaded window on the left-hand side, and we often see the same tiled floor and heavy tapestry table-cloth. On the walls behind are Vermeer's maps, revealing his interest in the world, an interest common to all Dutch people in that age of exploration and discovery.

All his pictures are painted in perfect colour harmonies, with wonderfully balanced and rather geometrical compositions. Each object is painted with loving care, and with such realism that one is reminded of "*Trompe d'Oeil*" painting. "*Trompe d'Oeil*" pictures are taken to such extremes of realism that the eye is deceived into thinking that the objects are really there.

* *See the Ladybird book "The Story of Music."*

Vermeer in his studio.

Few of Vermeer's drawings survive and, though pleasant, they bear no comparison with the magnificent drawings of Rubens and Rembrandt.

To produce his faultless paintings, Vermeer sometimes used an apparatus known as the 'camera-obscura'. Many artists of those times used this device, which was quite simple, consisting of a box with a small hole at the front and a ground-glass screen at the back. A hood, attached to the box, covered the artist's head. The scene in front of the camera was then visible on the glass screen, and the artist could outline the images. This tracing could then be transferred to a canvas ready for painting. The process must have been difficult and tedious, especially with the simpler type of camera, where the image would have been upside-down.

We have no record to show us the exact type of apparatus used by Vermeer, but are concerned only with the effect it had on his works. The picture opposite shows how the image on the glass screen has exaggerated the perspective. The figures are smaller, behind an enormous table, whilst the floor sweeps towards the viewer. Only because Vermeer was such a master of colour and detail was he able to create a masterpiece from this composition. Not all Vermeer's paintings reveal the use of the camera-obscura so vividly, but this picture, which is owned by Queen Elizabeth II, shows that he did use this method.

Vermeer using the camera-obscura.

It is sad to know that Vermeer's paintings were not greatly appreciated during his lifetime. In 1663 a French nobleman, Balthazar de Monconys, visited Delft, and stated: "I saw the painter Vermeer, who had none of his work with him, but we saw one at the house of a baker, bought for 600 florins. I should have thought it expensive at six pistoles". A pistole was a small Spanish coin, and shows how little de Monconys thought of Vermeer's work.

It may surprise us today that Vermeer's paintings were so little appreciated in his time. However, if we compare them with the work of his contemporaries, we can understand this more easily. Most Dutch "*genre*" pictures, apart from their purely pictorial values, contain little incidents or stories, such as a servant who has fallen asleep, or a naughty child; or they may moralise about the plight of poverty or other aspects of life. Vermeer's pictures depend upon their pictorial values alone. He shows us the beauty of one colour against another, smooth textures against rough ones. He built up his pictures into almost geometrical designs, balancing a dark shape in one part of his composition with another. These are known as "abstract qualities," and in this respect Vermeer was too far ahead of his time to be understood.

Another aspect of Vermeer's pictures which may not have been to the liking of his contemporaries, was the effect of the camera-obscura. Today we are so used to the effect of the camera that we scarcely notice it in Vermeer's work. But in his time people did notice it, and one critic declared ". . . the effect of the camera is striking but false."

de Monconys disapproves of a painting by Vermeer bought by the baker.

During his lifetime, Vermeer never achieved the success which Rembrandt enjoyed at the beginning of his career and Rubens enjoyed throughout his life.

He carried on his art-dealer's business, and a record reveals the good opinion held of him as an expert. An Amsterdam dealer had sold some pictures to the Elector of Brandenburg for a high price. The Elector was unhappy about them and sought Vermeer's opinion. Vermeer declared the pictures worthless.

In 1672 the King of France declared war on the Netherlands, and Vermeer's business suffered. He had to leave his house in the market square and move to a smaller dwelling.

He died in 1675, at the age of forty-three, leaving his wife and eight children to face bankruptcy. Poor Catharina had to pay the baker with two of his paintings, and twenty others were taken to settle money owed to a woman shopkeeper. In the end Catharina managed to free Vermeer's estate from debt.

Vermeer left about forty paintings. Although practically forgotten for two hundred years, he had at least one champion. Sir Joshua Reynolds, the first president of our Royal Academy, visited Holland in the middle of the eighteenth century, and declared Vermeer's "*Servant Pouring Milk*" (see p.47) the finest thing he saw there.

His genius was not recognised until the nineteenth century, when the French Impressionists began to work with similar ideas. Today his pictures are very popular.

Catharina on the way to settle debts, with Vermeer's paintings.

Vermeer painted comparatively few pictures, and collectors and art galleries have always been anxious to possess them. There is a fascinating true story of some forgeries which Van Meegeren, a Dutch painter, made of Vermeer's work between 1935 and 1945.

Van Meegeren was annoyed because his own paintings were scorned by the critics, and set to work to produce some forged 'Vermeers.' After many experiments he managed to produce very hard paint, which is typical of very old paintings, and he then worked on ancient canvas from which he had removed the original picture. He made Vermeer's blues from lapis-lazuli, a semi-precious stone, and ground the yellows from clay and resin. His pictures deceived everybody, and the first was sold to the Boyman's Museum in Rotterdam, for £60,000. In all, Van Meegeren produced six 'Vermeers' and received half-a-million pounds!

Field-Marshal Goering, a Nazi leader, managed to obtain Van Meegeren's sixth 'Vermeer.' The climax to this extraordinary story came after the war, when the picture was found among Goering's possessions, and Van Meegeren was arrested for collaborating with the enemy. Rather than admit to being a traitor, Van Meegeren confessed that the picture was a forgery. To prove his case he painted yet another 'Vermeer' in front of witnesses. Van Meegeren was sentenced to a year's imprisonment, but was allowed to go home, where he died shortly afterwards.

The story caused a tremendous stir, and Van Meegeren's forgeries were perhaps the greatest hoax of all time.

 Van Meegeren forges a Vermeer.

VERMEER
SENSATION

ENGLAND
NORTH SEA
Vermeer
Birthplace: Delft
Main place of work: Delft
Amsterdar
Haarlem
Leyden
Delft
Utr
Rotterdam
HOLLAN
Bruge
Antwerp
FLANDERS
Ghent
BELGIUM
Brussels
FRANCE
S
Rubens
Birthplace: Siegen
Main place of work: Antwerp